AUG 1 9 2016

W9-CMC-429

RETURN

Aaron Becker

CANDLEWICK PRESS

For my parents

Special thanks to Natalie Moss for her assistance with the petroglyph design in this book, and to *mis compañeros de erranT* in Granada, Spain, for opening their doors to an artist from far away.

Copyright © 2016 by Aaron Becker

All rights reserved. No part of this book may be reproduced, transmitted, or stored in an information retrieval system in any form or by any means, graphic, electronic, or mechanical, including photocopying, taping, and recording, without prior written permission from the publisher.

First edition 2016

Library of Congress Catalog Card Number 2015940258
ISBN 978-0-7636-7730-5

APS 21 20 19 18 17 16
10 9 8 7 6 5 4 3 2 1

Printed in Humen, Dongguan, China

The illustrations for this book were done in watercolor and pen and ink.

Candlewick Press
99 Dover Street
Somerville, Massachusetts 02144

visit us at www.candlewick.com

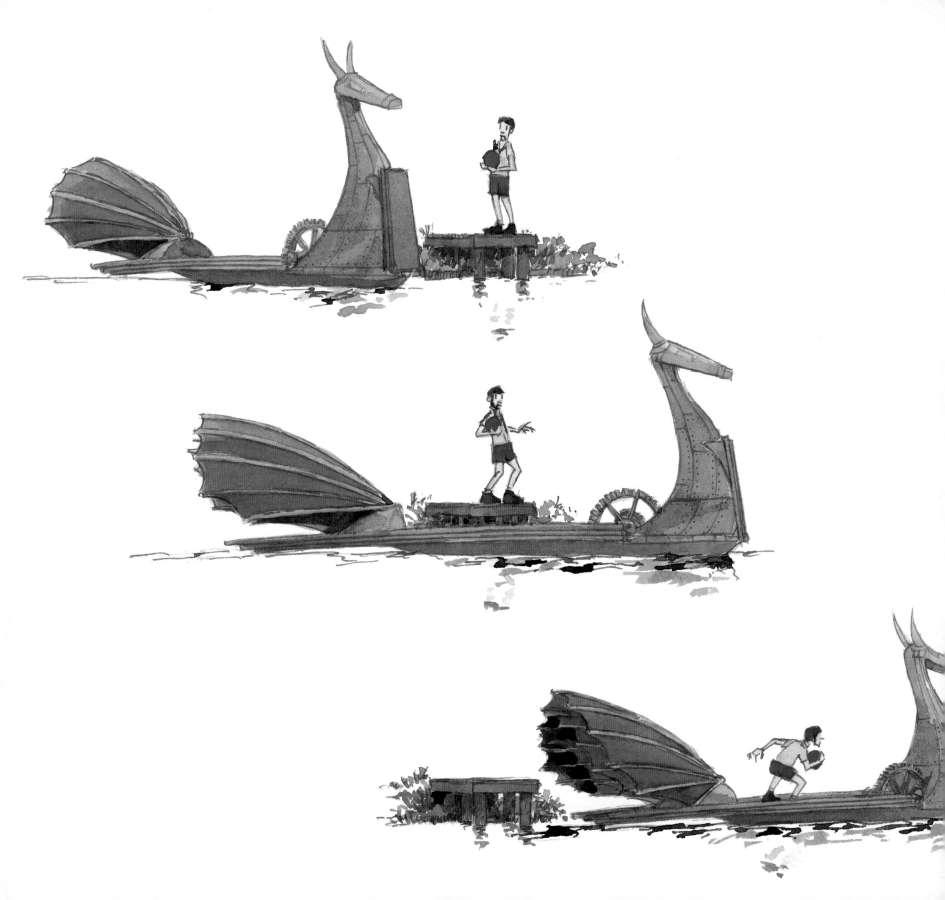